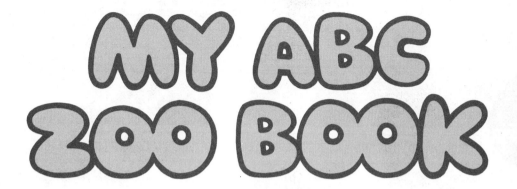

MY ABC ZOO BOOK

written by Kathy Downs
photography by Robert Cushman Hayes

© 1983, The STANDARD PUBLISHING Company, Cincinnati, Ohio
Division of STANDEX INTERNATIONAL Corporation. Printed in U.S.A.

S0-BOQ-955

Aa

Come with Lori's family for an alphabet trip
  through the zoo.
You'll see animals from A to Z that God made.
Alpaca is first with a shaggy fur coat.

"Do you know an animal for the letter B?" asked Dad.

"B is for bear," said Lori.

Lori laughed when she saw the bear in the water.

"Look, Eric! I think the other bear wants a turn."

Bb

Cc

"Here is a camel for letter C," said Mother.
"God made the camel to walk on desert sand.
He has strong legs and padded feet."
"I like his humps," said Lori.

"I found a deer for letter D," whispered Lori.
"Sh-sh. Deers can be very shy.
If we talk too loudly the deer will run and hide."

Dd

Ee

"Elephant is an animal that begins with E," said
  Mother.
"See the cute little baby, Eric," said Lori.
"I'm glad God gave her a mother that loves her just
  as our mother loves us."

Ff

"My favorite color is pink just like this bird," said
  Lori.
"That is a flamingo," said Dad.
"His long legs and neck help him catch fish to eat."

Gg

"What big eyes you have!" said Lori to the giraffe.
"G is the letter that begins your name.
Do your eyes help you see me when you are standing
   tall?"

"This animal has tiny eyes, but a big, big body,"
    said Dad.
"His name begins with H.
His name is almost as big as his body.
Can you say hippopotamus?"

Hh

"What animal begins with I?" asked Lori.
"This one does," said Mother.
"It looks like a goat and that begins with G," said
   Lori.
"It is a special goat called ibex," replied Mother.
"God made her so she can climb on rocks without
   falling."

Ii

Jj
Kk

"Here is an animal for two letters, J and K," said
   Mother.
"When this animal was a baby he was called a joey.
Now he is grown.
His name is kangaroo."

Ll

"Some animals are very loud like the lion for letter
    L," said Dad.
"Maybe he is hungry," said Lori.
"Let's ask the zoo keeper to bring him some lunch."

Mm

"Mother monkey, did the roaring lion scare your baby?" asked Lori.

"I'm sure all the animals are used to the noises at the zoo," said Mother.

"Monkey is our letter M."

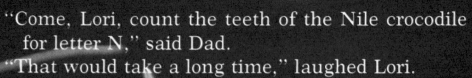

"Come, Lori, count the teeth of the Nile crocodile
   for letter N," said Dad.
"That would take a long time," laughed Lori.
"I hope he never has a toothache."

Nn

Oo

"Who-o-o is this wise-looking bird?" asked Mother.
"His name begins with O."
"That's easy," said Lori.
"He is an owl.
God gave him big eyes to see in the dark."

Pp

"P is for panda," said Dad.
"He is a special animal from China.
Very few pandas live in zoos.
Let's watch him eat.
His favorite food is bamboo."

"You'll have to look carefully to find the bird for the letter Q," Dad told Lori and Eric.

"God made it of special colors so it can hide in the grass."

"I see it!" said Lori.

"What's its name?"

"Quail," replied Dad.

Qq

Rr

"Look, everybody! There's a raccoon for the letter R.
Dad, do you think he is in trouble?" asked Lori.
"He's okay," said Dad.
"God gave him fingers to help him climb trees."

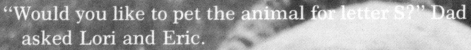

"Would you like to pet the animal for letter S?" Dad
    asked Lori and Eric.
"Their fuzzy wool gives us warm clothes."
"Yes, I would like to pet the sheep," answered Lori
    and Eric.

Ss

Tt

"There's an animal that looks just like our new
  kitten," said Lori.
"This is a tiger for letter T," said Mother.
"Do tigers purr like our kitten?" asked Lori.
"Yes," said Mother.

"Does this ugly bird have a name?" asked Lori.
"It is a vulture. It begins with the letter V.
He may not be pretty like the flamingo, but God
cares for him, too," answered Dad.

Uu
Vv

Ww

"W is the beginning letter for another bird," said Mother.
"The wood duck spends much time in the water. His special feathers keep him from getting too wet."

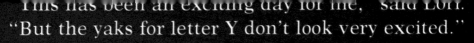

This has been an exciting day for me," said Lori.

"But the yaks for letter Y don't look very excited."

"Maybe they have had a long day at the zoo and are
    tired," said Mother.

"Aren't you tired, Lori?"

Xx Yy

"No," said Lori.
"I want to see the animal for letter Z."
"Well, here are the zebras," said Dad.
"Now we have seen the animals from A to Z.
Let's thank God for all the wonderful animals He
    has made."

Zz